The Stranded Whale

To Jason, Joanne,
and their twins, Amelia and Caroline,
who love the water
J. Y.

To Marianne, my lovely mother
and kitchen dancing partner
M. C.

Text copyright © 2015 by Jane Yolen
Illustrations copyright © 2015 by Melanie Cataldo

First edition 2015

Library of Congress Catalog Card Number 2014951789
ISBN 978-0-7636-6953-9

15 16 17 18 19 20 TWP 10 9 8 7 6 5 4 3 2 1

Printed in Johor Bahru, Malaysia

This book was typeset in Souvenir.
The illustrations were done in digital paint, oil paint, and pencil.

Candlewick Press
99 Dover Street
Somerville, Massachusetts 02144

visit us at www.candlewick.com

The Stranded Whale

JANE YOLEN

illustrated by MELANIE CATALDO

CANDLEWICK PRESS

SEPTEMBER 1971

We were walking home from school,
hurrying along the top of the dunes
because Ma always hates when we're late for supper.

Martin had basketball practice. Josh had stayed after school

for extra help in math. Long division is hard, he says. I say it's easy.

I needed to use the encyclopedia for a project about our state.

The last bus had already gone, so we had to walk,

but since there were three of us, it wasn't too bad.

Even hurrying, Josh took time to joke about how short I am.

He thinks because he's a minute older than me

he can talk that way.

We came to the big bend where you can see across the inlet
to the roof of our house and our boat beyond,
meaning Dad was already heading home from fishing.
The tide was going out, so he'd be hurrying, too.

The boys began running around me in circles,
singsonging my name, "Sally, Sally, in the alley . . ."
so I was the only one looking forward
and the first to see it.

Ahead on the beach was this big gray thing,
humped up on the drying sand.
This being Maine, the beach is full of boulders,
but that was no rock.

"Look!" I cried, pointing.

Both the boys turned at once, seeing what I saw:
a stranded whale lying on its side,
with the outgoing tide too far behind it
so it couldn't get back to the water on its own.

Running, slipping down the dune,
I stripped off my shoes, book bag, sweater,
leaving the bag and shoes on the sand.
As I ran toward the ocean,
it must have looked like I
was chasing the water,
which was fast heading out to the east.
I ran past beached starfish,
past little transparent jellyfish
breathing in and out on the sand,
past busy little crabs going
from tide pool to tide pool.
When I got to the water at last,
I plunged the sweater in
till it was completely soaked.
The water was a shock, so cold.
I could smell the brine.

I ran to the whale.
It stank of fear and deep water.
I wrung the sweater out on the whale's side,
then placed the wet bulk under its eye.

The boys chased off to the ocean as well,
dipped their sweaters in, ran back,
to place them on the whale's tail, on its fins.

The whale's eye, the size of a bicycle tire,
turned towards us.
It looked like it was weeping.

We had a whole ocean of water,
but I was afraid that it wouldn't be enough.

"We need help," I said.
Josh raced off, to an emergency phone
halfway along the beach,
maybe half a mile away.
The policeman who answered
said he'd call the Coast Guard,
though it took them twenty minutes
to get to us,
so we kept wetting down that whale
one sweater, two sweaters at a time.

Help arrived in a big blue camper bus
with swirls and slogans painted along its side,
followed by three pickup trucks.
The moon was just starting
to climb over the horizon.
Nine men and a woman named Eve
leaped out of the bus and trucks
like clowns from the circus.

"Good job, kids," one man called,
though we hadn't done all that much.

Then the men rocked and pushed the whale
back and forth toward the outgoing tide
Martin and Josh tried to help.
Eve shook her head and said to me,
"That's Leviathan, the great whale in the Bible.
They won't be moving it very far."

She was right. They hardly moved it an inch.
And by the time they quit rocking,
the ocean was even farther away
and the whale even more tired than the men.

Josh came back and stood by me.
He had tears in his eyes.
Not me. I was too mad to cry.
Mad at the unforgiving ocean,
rushing away from the shore.
Mad at our short arms
and the whale's long body.
Mad that we didn't have a boat, a winch,
long ropes to pull it into the sea.
Mad at everything.

The grown-ups hauled more water,
in big steel buckets from the Coast Guard truck,
and pots and pans from the camper.
None of it was enough.

Eve drove the camper into town
and came back with sandwiches and soda pop.
A bunch more cars followed after her,
all come to help, or so they said.
Everyone ate and drank like it was a party,
standing or squatting right next
to the whale's flukes or tail
all the while soaking it with water.

I had a sip of Josh's pop,

then went back to talk to the whale,

into the eye like it was an ear,

telling the whale how it was beautiful and strong,

how we would miss it, whatever happened next.

At last, though, just as the sun was setting,

the whale shut its great eye.

It gave out a huge sigh

like wind off the ocean.

The sigh smelled like seaweed,

like lobsters in Dad's traps,

like gutted fish on the pier.

And then it was gone, just like that.

I wondered how that whale—so big when it was alive—

could suddenly seem so much smaller, now that it was dead.

Didn't make any sense, but there it was.

I held Josh's hand all the way home,
or maybe he held mine.
Martin trotted ahead of us, to let Ma know
we were coming, why we were late.

Ma was mad because supper had gone stone cold,
so mad she was crying and couldn't catch her breath.
Papa could have whupped us for staying out so late.
But he didn't, just put his arms around us, saying,
"It's all right, kids, it's all right."
His clothes were damp from being out all day in his boat,
and he smelled like the sea.

Just then, the Coast Guard man came by.
He gave Josh, Martin, and me each a brown medal
with a picture of a whale on one side,
ocean waves on the other.

"You never covered the blowhole," he said,
as if he thought it the highest praise.

But why would we have done that?
Last year Grandpa died trying to catch his breath,
and suddenly I remembered him telling me once
that a whale's just a man writ large.
I sure wouldn't have covered Grandpa's nose,
his blowhole he used to call it as a joke.

So, the whale died and we were heroes.
Yet somehow I was still mad.
I put my medal in the drawer
and never took it out again.

I'd have given that old medal back
in a Portland instant
just to see old Leviathan alive again,
swimming joyously out to sea,
spouting through its blowhole,
tail slapping against the water,
black eyes shining.
I'd give that medal back for good
if I could see it one time
heading out to deep water,
lifting its tail, and diving deep,
and free.

Author's Note

I began this book on the coast of Scotland, where I spend summers. That day I'd heard there'd been a mass beaching of porpoises some twenty minutes from my house.

At first I set the story in our time and in Scotland, but soon realized that such beachings (of whales, dolphins, or porpoises) weren't confined to any time or place. In fact, whale beachings have been recorded as far back as 300 BCE.

More important for the story, the use of modern cell phones would have brought help sooner. Possibly with modern Coast Guard techniques, the whale might have been saved. At the very least, there'd have been crews of TV reporters and photographers complicating the effort.

It's important for the story that despite their best efforts, the children have to watch the whale die. Because the truth is that the majority of such strandings *do* end in death, and while it seems like an awful tragedy to anyone witnessing it, about 2,000 whales are found on beaches each year. Beachings are always sad, and many may have been avoidable, but the good news is that they don't affect whale species as a whole.

Sometimes a seemingly stranded whale has already died a natural death, and its carcass has simply washed ashore. Most whales do die in the water, sinking to the ocean bottom, where they become part of the local ecosystem. This is called "whale fall."

Why do whales beach? Beachings may be due to bad weather, or to a whale's already being sick or old, or because a group of whales has become infected with pneumonia, a virus, brain lesions, or parasites. Underwater volcanic activity—seaquakes— may play a part, as well as human-made ocean pollution. Collisions with large ships can take a toll. Even whales hunting too close to shore may be a cause. And some experts feel that recent military sonar stations may confuse the whales' own echolocation systems. There are many possibilities.

I'd like to think that when my young narrator grows up, she'll be the first in her family to go to college. Perhaps she'll study marine biology, working at the biological laboratory at Woods Hole, in Massachusetts. I visited there in the 1970s, and I think it would suit her perfectly.

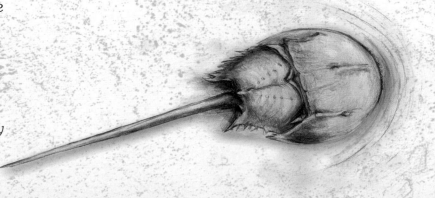

So, the whale died and we were heroes.
Yet somehow I was still mad.
I put my medal in the drawer
and never took it out again.

I'd have given that old medal back
in a Portland instant
just to see old Leviathan alive again,
swimming joyously out to sea,
spouting through its blowhole,
tail slapping against the water,
black eyes shining.
I'd give that medal back for good
if I could see it one time
heading out to deep water,
lifting its tail, and diving deep,
and free.

Author's Note

I began this book on the coast of Scotland, where I spend summers. That day I'd heard there'd been a mass beaching of porpoises some twenty minutes from my house.

At first I set the story in our time and in Scotland, but soon realized that such beachings (of whales, dolphins, or porpoises) weren't confined to any time or place. In fact, whale beachings have been recorded as far back as 300 BCE.

More important for the story, the use of modern cell phones would have brought help sooner. Possibly with modern Coast Guard techniques, the whale might have been saved. At the very least, there'd have been crews of TV reporters and photographers complicating the effort.

It's important for the story that despite their best efforts, the children have to watch the whale die. Because the truth is that the majority of such strandings *do* end in death, and while it seems like an awful tragedy to anyone witnessing it, about 2,000 whales are found on beaches each year. Beachings are always sad, and many may have been avoidable, but the good news is that they don't affect whale species as a whole.

Sometimes a seemingly stranded whale has already died a natural death, and its carcass has simply washed ashore. Most whales do die in the water, sinking to the ocean bottom, where they become part of the local ecosystem. This is called "whale fall."

Why do whales beach? Beachings may be due to bad weather, or to a whale's already being sick or old, or because a group of whales has become infected with pneumonia, a virus, brain lesions, or parasites. Underwater volcanic activity—seaquakes—may play a part, as well as human-made ocean pollution. Collisions with large ships can take a toll. Even whales hunting too close to shore may be a cause. And some experts feel that recent military sonar stations may confuse the whales' own echolocation systems. There are many possibilities.

I'd like to think that when my young narrator grows up, she'll be the first in her family to go to college. Perhaps she'll study marine biology, working at the biological laboratory at Woods Hole, in Massachusetts. I visited there in the 1970s, and I think it would suit her perfectly.

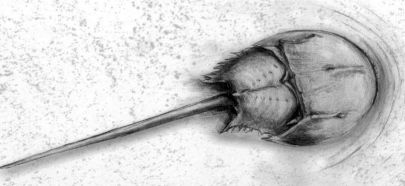